# WALLY THE GREEN MONSTER AND HIS WORLD TOUR

## Jerry Remy
### Illustrated by Danny Moore

MASCOT BOOKS
www.mascotbooks.com

Wally The Green Monster first appeared at a Red Sox game during the 1997 baseball season.

*Wally The Green Monster* was enjoying another season as the mascot for the *Boston Red Sox*. Wally decided that the All-Star break was the perfect time to take a trip around the world. He planned to visit fascinating places and meet many *Red Sox* fans along the way.

With his passport in hand, Wally left *Fenway Park* in a luxurious limousine and headed to Boston's Logan Airport. At the airport, Wally placed his red shoes through the x-ray machine and walked through the airport terminal.

Airport workers were thrilled to see the world-famous mascot. They cheered, "Hello, Wally! Where are you off to this time?"

Logan International Airport is one of America's busiest airports.

Greater Boston is the 10th largest metropolitan area in America.

Wally boarded his private jet and settled into his cozy seat. He knew that this would be a very long journey and was excited to get underway. The jet zoomed down the runway at Logan Airport and lifted high into the sky. The mascot enjoyed spectacular views of the Boston skyline. He even spied Fenway Park down below. "Good bye, Boston!" thought the mascot.

Wally finally arrived at his first stop—Ireland. From the capital city of Dublin, Wally drove through the beautiful Irish countryside to the famous Blarney Castle. A gentleman spotted the friendly mascot and said, "Hello, Wally! Welcome to Ireland." To celebrate his arrival, Wally climbed to the top of the castle and kissed the famous Blarney Stone for good luck. Feeling lucky, Wally dressed in a kilt and played the bagpipes. "Well done, Wally!" said onlookers.

FISH N CHIPS

From Ireland, it was a short trip to London, England. Wally had heard about the famous "fish and chips" served in England, so he stopped at a local restaurant to try for himself. "Delicious!" thought Wally.

Buckingham Palace is the home of the British monarchy.

Big Ben is part of the Palace of Westminster in London.

Next, it was time to go sightseeing in London. Wally stopped at Buckingham Palace, where he spotted Red Sox fans. The fans said, "Cheerio, Wally!" Big Ben was Wally's next stop. At Big Ben, Wally noticed it was time to make his way to his next destination!

From England, Wally traveled to France by train through the English Channel Tunnel. The train took the mascot through the French countryside before stopping in France's capital city, Paris. Wally arrived in France in time for the famous Tour de France, the world's best known bicycle race. Wally hopped on a bike and peddled to victory. Along the way, his fans cheered, "Go, Wally, go!"

*The Eiffel Tower, completed in 1889, was named for Gustave Eiffel, the tower's designer and engineer.*

Next, it was time to head to the Eiffel Tower. Wally was so impressed by the structure, he decided to paint it. "Bonjour, Wally!" said his friends.

*The Netherlands are well-known for their windmills and tulip fields.*

*Located in southeast Germany, Bavaria is the largest state in Germany.*

From Paris, Wally continued in Europe by heading north to The Netherlands. The mascot stopped at a windmill and admired the fields of fresh flowers. Wally's Dutch fans cheered, "Hello, Wally!"

In Germany, Wally visited a Bavarian village, where he was greeted by a musician playing an alpine horn. The musician called, "Guten Tag, Wally!"

*Located in Rome, the Coliseum was constructed nearly 2,000 years ago and once held 50,000 spectators.*

Wally's adventures took him next to Rome, Italy. Wally was inspired by the Roman Coliseum. He thought that it would be great fun to watch a Red Sox game there. He took a tour and learned all about the Coliseum's rich history and the events that were held there so long ago. The mascot even dressed in Roman Gladiator attire. Fans nearby said, "You are so brave, Wally!"

Wally continued to another famous Italian landmark—the Leaning Tower of Pisa. Not surprisingly, Wally ran into more Red Sox fans at the crooked tower. Posing for a picture as if he was holding the tower up, Wally made everyone laugh!

*The Leaning Tower of Pisa began leaning soon after it was constructed in 1173.*

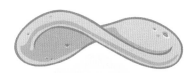

After a busy day of sightseeing in Italy, Wally was hungry. He stopped at a pizzeria and learned how to toss pizza dough high in the air. After several attempts, the mascot finally got the hang of it. The chef cheered, "Ciao, Wally!"

*The Pyramids of Giza are located near Cairo, Egypt, and were constructed over 4,500 years ago.*

Wally headed south to the continent of Africa. In Egypt, the mascot explored the Great Pyramids of Giza. Wally toured the grounds with an archeologist who told the mascot many fascinating facts about the pyramids and how they were made many, many years ago. The archeologist said, "Hello, Wally!"

Continuing south along the Nile River, Wally's next stop was a lively African market in Kenya. Wally was amazed at the beauty of the hand-made items that were for sale. He picked up several gifts for Red Sox players before continuing on his way.

Wally traveled to Tanzania for an African safari. Venturing onto the Serengeti was a thrill as he was able to observe amazing wildlife in their natural habitat. Wally felt a little nervous when he came across some big cats. A lion roared, "Hello, Wally!"

The Taj Mahal is located in Agra, India.

From Africa, it was a long journey to Asia, Wally's next stop. In India, Wally visited the Taj Mahal. Wally toured the grounds and learned that the mansion was built by an emperor in memory of his beloved wife. A tour guide welcomed Wally to India and said, "Namaste, Wally!"

*Cricket was first played in England around the year 1600 and is now played in more than 100 countries.*

In India, Wally tried his hand at cricket, another sport played with a bat-and-ball. Wally discovered that, unlike baseball, there were only two bases in this sport and games could sometimes last for days.

Wally's next stop was Nepal, a small country just north of India. With the help of a skilled guide, Wally scaled to the summit of Mount Everest, the world's tallest mountain. "Way to climb, Wally!" said the mountain guide.

*Located in Nepal, Mount Everest is the tallest mountain in the world with the summit at 29,035 feet above sea level.*

*The Great Wall of China stretches over 4,000 miles.*

The mascot's next stop was the Great Wall of China. Wally was amazed at how the wall seemed to go on forever. Wally walked…and walked…and walked until he tired himself out. Along the way, the mascot ran into his Chinese fans. They cheered, "Ni hao, Wally!"

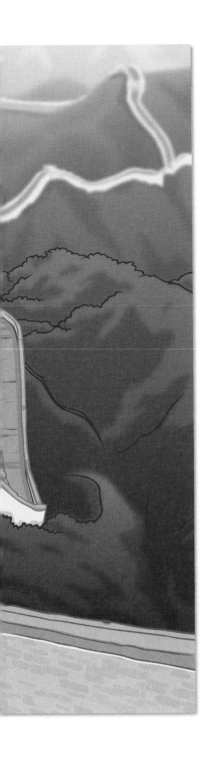

In Hong Kong, Wally set sail aboard a boat in Victoria Harbor, where he enjoyed spectacular views of Hong Kong's magnificent skyline.

Continuing in Asia, Wally's next stop was Tokyo, Japan. Wally toured the streets of Tokyo and marveled at how busy it was. Wally ran into Red Sox fans everywhere! "Konnichiwa, Wally!" they cheered!

*The Greater Tokyo Area, with a population of 35,000,000 people, is the world's most populous metropolitan area.*

It was time for Wally to get sporty. He wanted to watch a Sumo wrestling match, but soon found himself in the ring against a fierce Japanese warrior. Wally tried his best, but lost the match. His opponent said, "Nice try, Wally!"

*Sumo wrestling in Japan dates back over 2,000 years.*

Wally knew that baseball was popular in Japan, so he joined a Red Sox scout at a baseball game. The Red Sox were watching a famous Japanese pitcher the team hoped to bring to Boston next season. "He sure would look good in a Red Sox uniform!" said the baseball scout.

*Baseball was first played in Japan in 1878 and is today one of the most popular sports in the country.*

After the game, Wally clowned around with the Japanese team's mascot. He wasn't sure what kind of mascot he was, but he sure made Wally laugh. The mascot said to Wally, "Let's go, Red Sox!"

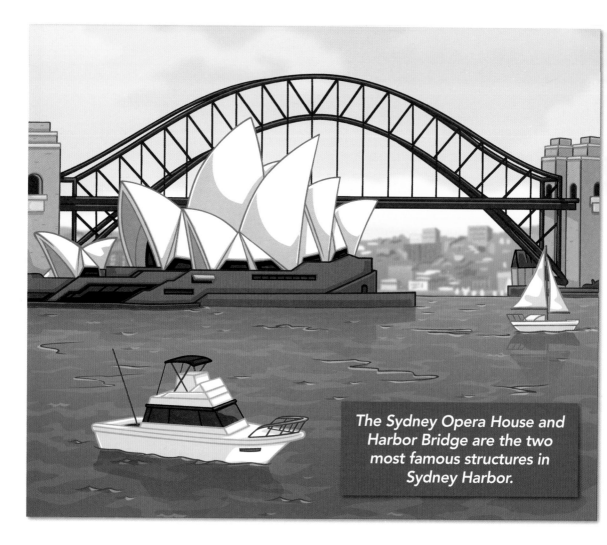

*The Sydney Opera House and Harbor Bridge are the two most famous structures in Sydney Harbor.*

Wally The Green Monster continued "down under" to Australia. At Sydney Harbor, Wally enjoyed views of the world-famous Sydney Harbor Bridge and the Sydney Opera House aboard a yacht.

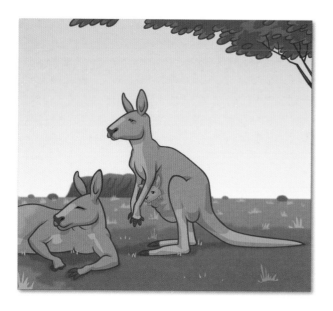

In the Australian Outback, Wally came across spectacular wildlife, including kangaroos and Koala bears. Wally's tour guide called, "G'day Wally! Welcome to Australia!"

*Kangaroos are native to the continent of Australia.*

Wally grabbed his diving gear and dove into the South Pacific Ocean along the Great Barrier Reef, where he observed amazing marine life. A green sea turtle spotted the mascot and snapped, "Hello, Wally!"

*The Great Barrier Reef, off Australia's northeast coast, is the largest coral reef system in the world.*

From Australia, Wally flew over the Pacific Ocean to South America. In Brazil, the mascot joined the national soccer team. Wally amazed his teammates with his soccer skills as he kicked a game-winning goal. "Goooaaaal, Wally!" cheered his teammates as they celebrated the victory.

Wally paddled down the Amazon River, stopping along the way to visit his friends and fans. "Hello, Wally!" cheered his fans.

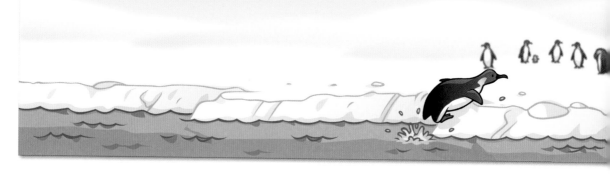

*Soccer is believed to be the most popular sport in the world.*

Wally traveled all the way to the southern tip of South America, where he boarded a boat for a journey to Antarctica, the last of the seven continents on Wally's journey around the world. Wally bundled up and joined a group of penguins as they waddled across the ice. The penguins said, "Hello, Wally!"

*Located over the South Pole, Antarctica is the fifth largest continent in the world, and is home to many penguins.*

*Evidence of the Mayan civilization can be found in parts of Mexico.*

Wally headed back to North America, all the way to Mexico. He admired ancient Mayan structures and was interested to learn how they were built. "Hola, Wally!" cheered fellow sightseers.

Next, Wally traveled across the Caribbean Sea before stopping at the Dominican Republic. Wally knew that several famous Red Sox players were born in the Dominican Republic. He also knew that baseball was played in sandlots all over the island. Wally visited a game and joined a Red Sox scout as they watched the talented youngsters. One kid, wearing a Red Sox jersey, said, "Hello, Wally!"

Dominican Republic has produced more Major League Baseball players than any other country, besides the United States.

Knowing his vacation was winding down, Wally found a beach, where he soaked up the sun. He had a fun trip, but he knew that it was time to go home.

Finally, Wally made it back to Boston and his home at Fenway Park. He climbed into his warm, cozy bed and started to think about his travels and of all the nice people he had met along the way. As Wally drifted off to sleep, he thought, "Go, Red Sox!"

Good night, Wally.

To my favorite Wally fan, my grandson, Dominik.
—Jerry Remy

This one goes out to all my peeps in the
Southeastern Hemisphere. You know who you are!
—Danny Moore

For more information about our products,
please visit us online at www.mascotbooks.com.

For more information, please contact Mascot Books,
P.O. Box 220157, Chantilly, VA 20153-0157

ISBN: 1-934878-49-9

Printed in the United States.

www.mascotbooks.com

**MASCOT BOOKS**
www.mascotbooks.com

**Baseball**

| | | |
|---|---|---|
| Boston Red Sox | Hello, *Wally*! | Jerry Remy |
| Boston Red Sox | *Wally The Green Monster And His Journey Through Red Sox Nation*! | Jerry Remy |
| Boston Red Sox | Coast to Coast with *Wally The Green Monster* | Jerry Remy |
| Boston Red Sox | A Season with *Wally The Green Monster* | Jerry Remy |
| Colorado Rockies | Hello, *Dinger*! | Aimee Aryal |
| Detroit Tigers | Hello, *Paws*! | Aimee Aryal |
| New York Yankees | Let's Go, *Yankees*! | Yogi Berra |
| New York Yankees | *Yankees* Town | Aimee Aryal |
| New York Mets | Hello, *Mr. Met*! | Rusty Staub |
| New York Mets | *Mr. Met* and his Journey Through the Big Apple | Aimee Aryal |
| St. Louis Cardinals | Hello, *Fredbird*! | Ozzie Smith |
| Philadelphia Phillies | Hello, *Phillie Phanatic*! | Aimee Aryal |
| Chicago Cubs | Let's Go, *Cubs*! | Aimee Aryal |
| Chicago White Sox | Let's Go, *White Sox*! | Aimee Aryal |
| Cleveland Indians | Hello, *Slider*! | Bob Feller |
| Seattle Mariners | Hello, *Mariner Moose*! | Aimee Aryal |
| Washington Nationals | Hello, *Screech*! | Aimee Aryal |
| Milwaukee Brewers | Hello, *Bernie Brewer*! | Aimee Aryal |

**College**

| | | |
|---|---|---|
| Alabama | Hello, Big Al! | Aimee Aryal |
| Alabama | Roll Tide! | Ken Stabler |
| Alabama | Big Al's Journey Through the Yellowhammer State | Aimee Aryal |
| Arizona | Hello, Wilbur! | Lute Olson |
| Arizona State | Hello, Sparky! | Aimee Aryal |
| Arkansas | Hello, Big Red! | Aimee Aryal |
| Arkansas | Big Red's Journey Through the Razorback State | Aimee Aryal |
| Auburn | Hello, Aubie! | Aimee Aryal |
| Auburn | War Eagle! | Pat Dye |
| Auburn | Aubie's Journey Through the Yellowhammer State | Aimee Aryal |
| Boston College | Hello, Baldwin! | Aimee Aryal |
| Brigham Young | Hello, Cosmo! | LaVell Edwards |
| Cal - Berkeley | Hello, Oski! | Aimee Aryal |
| Clemson | Hello, Tiger! | Aimee Aryal |
| Clemson | Tiger's Journey Through the Palmetto State | Aimee Aryal |
| Colorado | Hello, Ralphie! | Aimee Aryal |
| Connecticut | Hello, Jonathan! | Aimee Aryal |
| Duke | Hello, Blue Devil! | Aimee Aryal |
| Florida | Hello, Albert! | Aimee Aryal |
| Florida | Albert's Journey Through the Sunshine State | Aimee Aryal |
| Florida State | Let's Go, 'Noles! | Aimee Aryal |
| Georgia | Hello, Hairy Dawg! | Aimee Aryal |
| Georgia | How 'Bout Them Dawgs! | Vince Dooley |
| Georgia | Hairy Dawg's Journey Through the Peach State | Vince Dooley |
| Georgia Tech | Hello, Buzz! | Aimee Aryal |
| Gonzaga | Spike, The Gonzaga Bulldog | Mike Pringle |
| Illinois | Let's Go, Illini! | Aimee Aryal |
| Indiana | Let's Go, Hoosiers! | Aimee Aryal |
| Iowa | Hello, Herky! | Aimee Aryal |
| Iowa State | Hello, Cy! | Amy DeLashmutt |
| James Madison | Hello, Duke Dog! | Aimee Aryal |
| Kansas | Hello, Big Jay! | Aimee Aryal |
| Kansas State | Hello, Willie! | Dan Walter |
| Kentucky | Hello, Wildcat! | Aimee Aryal |
| LSU | Hello, Mike! | Aimee Aryal |
| LSU | Mike's Journey Through the Bayou State | Aimee Aryal |
| Maryland | Hello, Testudo! | Aimee Aryal |
| Michigan | Let's Go, Blue! | Aimee Aryal |
| Michigan State | Hello, Sparty! | Aimee Aryal |
| Michigan State | Sparty's Journey Through Michigan | Aimee Aryal |
| Middle Tennessee | Hello, Lightning! | Aimee Aryal |
| Minnesota | Hello, Goldy! | Aimee Aryal |
| Mississippi | Hello, Colonel Rebel! | Aimee Aryal |

**Pro Football**

| | | |
|---|---|---|
| Carolina Panthers | Let's Go, Panthers! | Aimee Aryal |
| Chicago Bears | Let's Go, Bears! | Aimee Aryal |
| Dallas Cowboys | How 'Bout Them Cowboys! | Aimee Aryal |
| Green Bay Packers | Go, Pack, Go! | Aimee Aryal |
| Kansas City Chiefs | Let's Go, Chiefs! | Aimee Aryal |
| Minnesota Vikings | Let's Go, Vikings! | Aimee Aryal |
| New York Giants | Let's Go, Giants! | Aimee Aryal |
| New York Jets | J-E-T-S! Jets, Jets, Jets! | Aimee Aryal |
| New England Patriots | Let's Go, Patriots! | Aimee Aryal |
| Pittsburg Steelers | Here We Go, Steelers! | Aimee Aryal |
| Seattle Seahawks | Let's Go, Seahawks! | Aimee Aryal |
| Washington Redskins | Hail To The Redskins! | Aimee Aryal |

**Basketball**

| | | |
|---|---|---|
| Dallas Mavericks | Let's Go, Mavs! | Mark Cuban |
| Boston Celtics | Let's Go, Celtics! | Aimee Aryal |

**Other**

| | | |
|---|---|---|
| Kentucky Derby | White Diamond Runs For The Roses | Aimee Aryal |
| Marine Corps Marathon | Run, Miles, Run! | Aimee Aryal |
| Mississippi State | Hello, Bully! | Aimee Aryal |
| Missouri | Hello, Truman! | Todd Donoho |
| Missouri | Hello, Truman! Show Me Missouri! | Todd Donoho |
| Nebraska | Hello, Herbie Husker! | Aimee Aryal |
| North Carolina | Hello, Rameses! | Aimee Aryal |
| North Carolina | Rameses' Journey Through the Tar Heel State | Aimee Aryal |
| North Carolina St. | Hello, Mr. Wuf! | Aimee Aryal |
| North Carolina St. | Mr. Wuf's Journey Through North Carolina | Aimee Aryal |
| Northern Arizona | Hello, Louie! | Jeanette S. Bake |
| Notre Dame | Let's Go, Irish! | Aimee Aryal |
| Ohio State | Hello, Brutus! | Aimee Aryal |
| Ohio State | Brutus' Journey | Aimee Aryal |
| Oklahoma | Let's Go, Sooners! | Aimee Aryal |
| Oklahoma State | Hello, Pistol Pete! | Aimee Aryal |
| Oregon | Go Ducks! | Aimee Aryal |
| Oregon State | Hello, Benny the Beaver! | Aimee Aryal |
| Penn State | Hello, Nittany Lion! | Aimee Aryal |
| Penn State | We Are Penn State! | Joe Paterno |
| Purdue | Hello, Purdue Pete! | Aimee Aryal |
| Rutgers | Hello, Scarlet Knight! | Aimee Aryal |
| South Carolina | Hello, Cocky! | Aimee Aryal |
| South Carolina | Cocky's Journey Through the Palmetto State | Aimee Aryal |
| So. California | Hello, Tommy Trojan! | Aimee Aryal |
| Syracuse | Hello, Otto! | Aimee Aryal |
| Tennessee | Hello, Smokey! | Aimee Aryal |
| Tennessee | Smokey's Journey Through the Volunteer State | Aimee Aryal |
| Texas | Hello, Hook 'Em! | Aimee Aryal |
| Texas | Hook 'Em's Journey Through the Lone Star State | Aimee Aryal |
| Texas A & M | Howdy, Reveille! | Aimee Aryal |
| Texas A & M | Reveille's Journey Through the Lone Star State | Aimee Aryal |
| Texas Tech | Hello, Masked Rider! | Aimee Aryal |
| UCLA | Hello, Joe Bruin! | Aimee Aryal |
| Virginia | Hello, CavMan! | Aimee Aryal |
| Virginia Tech | Hello, Hokie Bird! | Aimee Aryal |
| Virginia Tech | Yea, It's Hokie Game Day! | Frank Beame |
| Virginia Tech | Hokie Bird's Journey Through Virginia | Aimee Aryal |
| Wake Forest | Hello, Demon Deacon! | Aimee Aryal |
| Washington | Hello, Harry the Husky! | Aimee Aryal |
| Washington State | Hello, Butch! | Aimee Aryal |
| West Virginia | Hello, Mountaineer! | Aimee Aryal |
| West Virginia | The Mountaineer's Journey Through West Virginia | Leslie H. Han |
| Wisconsin | Hello, Bucky! | Aimee Aryal |
| Wisconsin | Bucky's Journey Through the Badger State | Aimee Aryal |